MAGGIE MAB AND THE BOGEY BEAST

Maggie Mab
and the Bogey Beast

Retold by **Valerie Scho Carey**

Illustrated by **Johanna Westerman**

Arcade Publishing ❧ *New York*

LITTLE, BROWN AND COMPANY

For my parents, Ira and Zelda, with love — V.S.C.

To my parents, who have been a great source
of encouragement and inspiration — J.W.

Text copyright © 1992 by Valerie Scho Carey
Illustrations copyright © 1992 by Johanna Westerman

First Edition

Library of Congress Cataloging-in-Publication Data
Carey, Valerie Scho.
  Maggie Mab and the bogey beast / retold by Valerie Scho Carey ;
illustrated by Johanna Westerman. — 1st ed.
    p.   cm.
Summary: A spirited adaptation of a traditional tale about a feisty,
good-natured old woman's run-in with the fabled bogey beast.
ISBN 1-55970-155-2
[1. Folklore — Great Britain.]   I. Westerman, Johanna, ill.   II. Title.
PZ8.1.C185Mag   1992
398.2 — dc20
[E]   91-18084

Published in the United States by Arcade Publishing, Inc.,
New York, a Little, Brown company

WOR
Designed by Marc Cheshire

*Published simultaneously in Canada by
Little, Brown & Company (Canada) Limited*

Printed in the United States of America
1 3 5 7 9 10 8 6 4 2

MAGGIE MAB AND THE BOGEY BEAST

T H E R E was an old woman who was poor as the sound
of a tin bell, but as kind and good-natured as ever a body
could be. The old woman, whose name was Maggie Mab, lived in
a tiny stone cottage so old that only the hills around could remem-
ber when it had been built. But she kept it neat as a chapel cleaned
for Sunday, and managed a garden, too.

She earned the few pennies to buy what she needed, and rarely anything more, by helping the good farmwives round about with errands and butter churning and baking and the like. And as little as she had for herself, and for true it seemed it was scarce little, the old woman was happy and always had a kind word and some tea for neighbor and stranger alike, and even a biscuit for the children who came to her door. So it was that while Maggie Mab might not have had enough of anything to scratch the itch of her wants, she wore a contented face and burdened no one with either her dreams or her troubles.

It happened one time that the old woman was kept later than usual helping a farmwife with chores. When at last she set off upon the road home, evening was fast slipping into night and shadows stretched everywhere long and dark. Maggie Mab knew, as everyone did, that the bogey beast was like to be hidden in those shadows, just waiting to play its tricks on unwary passersby. Sometimes its pranks were no more than a nuisance, like taking the shape of a farmer's favorite cow and kicking over the milk pails. Other times it was given to much greater meanness. The old woman shivered, recalling the story of how the wicked creature had taken the shape of a beautiful horse, enticed a wary traveler onto its back, and then plunged with him into a cold lake and drowned him. Maggie Mab knew these stories and more about the shape-shifting bogey beast, but they were less on her mind than the pleasure of a warm cup of tea and a well-earned rest. So she walked along in the glooming night with thoughts of the bogey beast only occasionally crisscrossing with thoughts of home.

"Phoof-now! What's this?" she cried when her foot struck against something hard. "Someone's left a great iron pot smack in the road. Careless they must have been to let the thing drop by the way and never bother to pick it up. Why, if it had been a cart come along instead of my old foot, there sure would have been a toppling-over of an accident."

Maggie Mab looked up and down the road for a sign of who might have left the pot lying there. But she saw nothing, not even the tracks from the wagon off which it might have tumbled. "More than likely," she said to herself, "any pot left in the road has a hole in it and is no good to anyone. But even such a pot could be useful. I could plant flowers in it and set it by the door to cheer me as I come and go." So she laid hold of the pot to carry it home with her.

"Strange-heavy it is for an old, empty pot," thought Maggie Mab. She lifted the lid and peeked in to see what it was that made it so heavy.

"Phoof-now! It's full of gold coins!" The old woman picked up one of the coins and bit it hard to see whether it was real. "If I leave the pot here, some thief is sure to make off with it. Wiser to take it home for safekeeping. Now mind, you are an honest woman, so it's your duty to return the pot to its owner if you can. But wouldn't it be lovely if no one claimed it! Could be it was dropped by a robber who daren't come out in the light and ask for it back. Or it fell off a gentleman's wagon, and he's so rich he'll never miss it. And if no one claims it, why shouldn't I keep it for myself? Now, there's cream for the cat!"

But the pot was too heavy for her to lift, so she tied her shawl about it and dragged it bumping along behind her toward home.

As she went, she thought of all the grand things she might do with gold pieces. "I might buy a great house and hire servants and live as the lords and ladies do. I could sip tea by a cozy fire and eat little sandwiches and cakes till I'm pleased to stop. Why, I might not ever have to work again! But lazy as a badger in winter and plump as a pincushion I've no wish to be. I might buy a patch of land with sheep and chickens to tend. Or maybe I'll bury the pot and draw out the gold as I need it, one piece at a time."

Dragging the pot and thinking of what she could do with the gold were heavy chores, so Maggie Mab stopped to rest and have

another look at her good fortune. "Phoof-now!" she cried, for wrapped in her shawl was no pot of gold at all but a great lump of silver. The silver shone so in the moonlight that the old woman hastily covered it. She rubbed her eyes and lifted the corner of the shawl to have another peek. "Sure I was that I had a pot of gold, but certain I am that it's a lump of silver now. I must have been dreaming. But silver is even better than gold. So many coins would have been hard to keep account of, and, anyway, coins are easily stolen. A great lump of silver will be much easier to keep safe." With that, she started off for home with the lump of silver in tow.

After a time, she tired again. She sat down beside her treasure to have a look at it. "Phoof-now!" she gasped. "My lump of silver has become a lump of iron!"

Maggie Mab scarce knew what to think. Her eyes had never played tricks on her.

"A long day's work and the lateness of the hour, that's what is making me see things all ajumble." She shook her head and folded the shawl over the iron. "A lump of iron is great luck to have," she said. "Better even than a lump of silver or a pot of gold. With gold or silver under my roof, I'd not sleep a wink for fear of robbers or murderers. But iron I can sell for pennies aplenty. Why, I'll have pennies to buy sweets and tea for all the neighbors and still have enough left over to keep me happy a good long while." She knotted her shawl around the iron and set off down the road.

But again she grew tired and stopped for a rest. When she looked in her shawl to be certain of the iron — "Phoof-now! My lump of iron has become an old stone!" True it was. She ran her hands over the stone that a short while before had been a great lump of iron with its promise of pennies. "Ah, well," she sighed, "'tis fortunate am I that I've found this old stone, for I've been needing one just such as this to hold open my gate."

Maggie Mab hauled the stone the rest of the way home. When she got to her gate, she stopped to unwrap it from her shawl and set it in its place.

"A fine gate-stone this will make," said the old woman, quite pleased. "It is smooth and round, with no roughness about it. One might even say it was beautiful."

No sooner had she set the stone down than it shivered and heaved and let out a great squeal! Up it popped into the air, growing bigger as it went, till it was the size of a large horse. Four bony legs sprang from beneath it, and a skinny neck with the head of a bogey and the long ears of an ass shot out from the top. The bogey beast kicked up its heels and whipped its tail around as Maggie Mab stood frozen to the spot with her hands still cupped as though holding the stone.

"Well, I never!" said Maggie Mab.

"Well, you have!" snorted the bogey beast, leaping and cavorting around her till she was so dizzy that her eyes wobbled. Then the creature gave a leap and a bawl and, stooping low, slipped the old woman onto its back.

Away they sped with Maggie Mab clenching the beast's scrawny mane in her fists. They skirted stone walls that twisted like snakes rippling over the hills in the dim owl-light. They raced along narrow paths that seemed barely to cling to the hillsides.

Out across the black water of a lake they flew. The wind brought tears to Maggie Mab's eyes, but she clung to the beast and called out, "This is far better than a stone! Who would have thought an old woman could fly!"

On and on through the night they sped, with the bogey beast braying madly as they went. The braying scraped against Maggie Mab's ears like chalk against slate. The beast rose high into the air, then plunged straight for the dark water. Maggie Mab clung desperately to its neck. Her skirts dragged in the pitchy waters that churned beneath her. White claws tipping the waves grasped and snatched at her legs. But she would say nothing to let the bogey beast know of her fear.

"What a kindness this cool water is to my tired feet," she called. "Luck, it seems, just has a way of finding me!"

The old woman's words were hardly spoken when she found herself back at the very gate from which she had started.

The bogey beast stared at her with its eyes of green light before breaking the silence that was between them:

Because not a word of complaint have you spake,
Unknot your shawl and give it a shake.

With that, the creature gave a last leap and bawl and disappeared down the road, laughing and braying as it went.

The old woman leaned against the gate to steady herself. Then she began to laugh, too. "Imagine that! I've hauled the bogey beast around in my shawl like an old sack of potatoes, and still I'm here to tell about it. Why, I do feel grand!" And as she knelt to pick up the shawl, three gold coins fell from its folds and landed *clink-clank-clunk* in the dust at her feet.

Maggie Mab picked up the coins, went into her cottage, and brewed herself some tea. She thought and thought about what she could best do with those coins, and what she thought of was what she did. With the first coin she bought chickens, wood for a coop, a ram and a ewe, and a plump milk cow. With these she could make her living and would never again have to run errands or do chores for someone else. With the second coin she bought some biscuits and cakes and all the trimmings for a glorious feast, and she invited all her neighbors to celebrate her good fortune.

The third coin she placed upon her mantel, but spend it she would not.

For many a year Maggie Mab looked to that lone coin to remind her of the night when gold had turned to silver, silver to iron, iron to stone, and stone to bogey. And on the back of the bogey, Maggie Mab had flown.